Get ready
for these hilarious jokes
from Mike Thaler!

- Who's pink and fat and drinks blood?
- What do you get if you put a pig in a blender?
- What does a little pig get twice a year from school?
- What famous pig monster is six feet tall and sewn together?

Don't stop yet—there's more to come!

OINKERS AWAY!

Pig Riddles, Cartoons and Jokes by Mike Thaler, America's Riddle King

A MINSTREL® BOOK

PUBLISHED BY POCKET BOOKS

New York   London   Toronto   Sydney   Tokyo

For Sara Heart Bacon
and
Mary Ham Arnold
who both love pigs

A MINSTREL PAPERBACK *ORIGINAL*

 A Minstrel Book published by
POCKET BOOKS, a division of Simon & Schuster Inc.
1230 Avenue of the Americas, New York, NY 10020

ISBN: 0-671-67456-0

First Minstrel Books printing January 1989

10 9 8 7 6 5 4 3 2 1

A MINSTREL BOOK and colophon are trademarks
of Simon & Schuster Inc.

Printed in the U.S.A.

GREAT AND FAMOUS PIGS

What famous pig was the father of psycho-hamalysis?

Pigmund Freud

What famous pig was the world's greatest painter?

Rembrandt van Swine

What pig was a famous Greek mathematician?

Pigthagorus

What pig was a famous Greek philosopher?

Sowcrates

What famous pig discovered relativity?

Albert Einswine

What two famous pig explorers discovered each other in Africa?

Stanley and Livingswine

What pig was a famous violinist?

Piggynini

What pig was the most famous artist of our age?

Pigcasso

Who is the pig's favorite rock star?

Cindy Slopper

What pig was a famous Indian maiden?

Porkahontas

What pig was a famous Russian pigtator?

Joseph Sty-in

What pig is a famous clothes designer?

Jacques Saswine

What famous sleepy pig chased Robin Hood?

The Sheriff of Nodding-ham

What famous pig is a missing link?

Pig Foot

DINING OUT

What kinds of pigs are these?

1.

2.

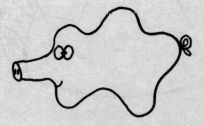

3.

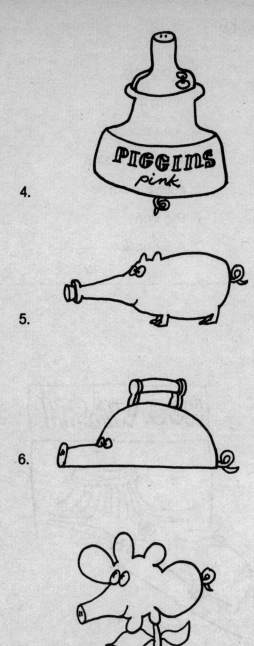

4.

5.

6.

7.

Hamswers

1. A pig pen

2. A pig ax

3. A hamoeba

4. A bottle of oink

5. A swine bottle

6. Pig Iron

7. A pigonia

PIG RIDDLES

What do you call it when the air
is full of pigs?

Sma-hog

What do you call a pig that keeps you dry when it rains?

A hambrella

What's it called when pigs eat lunch in the park?

A pignic

What do you call a book about a pig's life?

A bihography

Where do pigs go on vacation?

The Ba-ham-as

Where do pigs land their planes?

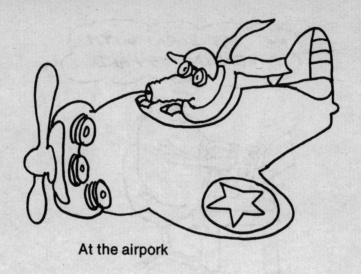

At the airpork

Do pigs drive cars?

No. They drive pig-up trucks.

Where do you put dirty pigs?

In a hamper

How do you take a pig to the hospital?

In a hambulance

What do pigs do when they meet?

They shake hams.

What do you call a pig that studies the past?

A hamthropologist

What do you call a prehistoric pig?

A be-ham-oth

What is the great pig beauty pageant from Hamlantic City?

Miss Hamerica

What does a little pig get twice a year from school?

Repork cards

What does a little pig get every night?

Hogs and kisses

What does a little pig put on every night?

Pigjamas

Where can you buy pigs' feet?

At a hock shop

What groups do little pigs join?

The cub snouts, the boy snouts
and the girl snouts

What famous lady is the symbol of Hamerica?

The Statue of Liboarty

What do pigs watch at night?

Smellavision

Why do pigs drink Coke?

Because "It's the Squeal Thing"

What is one of the piggest buildings in the world?

The Hampire State Building
in New Pork City

GEHOGRAPHY

What Chinese city has the most pigs?

Pig-king

What Alaskan city has the most pigs?

Oinkerage

In what city do pigs wear wooden shoes?

Hamsterdam

In what country are there many lady pigs?

Sowdi Arabia

What city in Hamerica has the most pigs?

Porkland, Oregham

What state in Hamerica has the most pigs?

Pen-swill-vania

What Hamerican river do most pigs sail on?

The Swinee River

**What two oceans are
in the Western Hamisphere?**

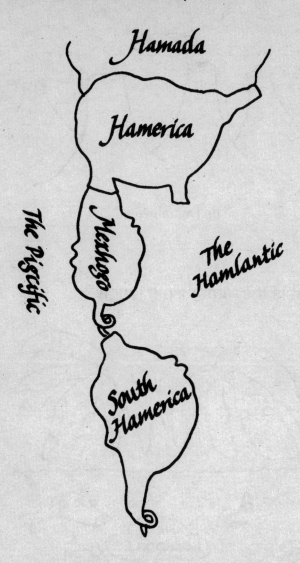

The Pigcific and the Hamlantic

What is the famous pig mountain range?

The Hamalayas

What is the famous pig jungle?

WE'RE HOCKODILES

The Hamazon

DINING OUT

THE OLYMPIGS

The Hog Step and Jump

The Pork Vault

The Hammer Throw

The Discus-ting Throw

And the Pen-tathlon

GREAT PIGS IN SPORTS

What pig hit
755 home runs?

Oink Aaron

What pig was the greatest
heavyweight boxing hampion ever?

Mudhamad Ali

What are the greatest professional pig football teams?

The Pigsburgh Squealers
The Los Angeles Hams
The Dallas Sowboys
The San Francisco Forty-Swiners
The Myhamy Dolphins
The Greenbay Hockers

Who was the greatest ice hoggy player ever?

Gordie Sow

What pig is a great figure skater?

Piggy Fleming

What are the favorite sports of pigs?

1.

2.

3.

4.

5.

6.

Hamswers

1. Pig Pong

2. Ham Ball

3. Sow-ker

4. Ice Hoggy

5. Skate Boaring

6. Hogging

PIG CROSSES

What do you get if you cross a pig with a camel?

A Hamel

A pig with a small dog?

A Piginese

A pig with a small fish?

A Hamchovy

A pig with a mouse?

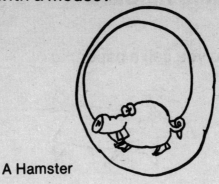

A Hamster

A pig with a frog?

A Hamphibian

A pig with a cactus?

A Porkupine

MORE PIG RIDDLES

What do you call a paper pig?

Orig-hami

What do you call a rich pig?

A swillionaire

What pig gets the most food?

The piggest

What do you call a pig
that takes shorthand?

A sty-hog-rapher

What little pig causes pigs to fall in love?

Cupig

How do pigs keep their boats in place?

With oinkers

What do pigs have above their feet?

Oinkles

What do lady pigs sit on?

Sowfas

What do you call a bunch of pigs standing around a little cottage?

A pigget fence

How did they kill Sowcrates?

They made him drink a cup of ham-lock.

Who's pink and fat and drinks blood?

Count Porkula

What's green and sour and goes oink?

A dill piggle

What's pink and goes ninety miles an hour?

A pig on roller skates

Why do pigs have lots of bread?

Because they're always bacon

Why are pigs always healthy?

Because they're always in the pink

What do pigs ride waves with?

A surf boar

What do you call it when a bunch of pigs jumps out and surprises you?

A hambush

What do you call a pig that steals wallets?

A pig-pocket

What does a pig get when his meter runs out?

A porking ticket

What magical kingdom had a lot of pigs?

Ham-a-lot

What do you call lady pigs in Mexico?

Sows of the boarder

What do you call a pig that fights bulls?

A pigador

What do you call a robot pig?

A cyboar

What do you get if you put a pig in a blender?

A ground hog

What do you call a pig in a lighthouse?

A bacon

PIG RHYMERS

1) What do you call a pig with a
   fat nose?

2) What do you call a frightened pig?

3) What do you call a pig wearing
   blond hair?

4) Who brings the baby pigs?

5) What do you call a pig's laugh?

6) What does a very clean pig have?

Hamswers

1) A stout snout

2) Shakin' bacon

3) A pig in a wig

4) The pork stork

5) A piggle giggle

6) A fine swine shine

PIG FAVORITES

What is the pig's favorite musical?

Oinklahoma
They also like *Pigadoon, Porky and Mess, Sows Pacific, Grease,* and *A Chorus Swine*

What is the pig's favorite opera?

Pigaro

What is the pig's all-time favorite ballet?

Swine Lake

What is a musical pig's favorite Instrument?

The glocken-squeal

Who is the pig's favorite war movie hero?

Hambo

What is the pig's favorite Beatle song?

"I Wanna Hold Your Ham"

What is the pig's favorite TV detective show?

Myhamy Vice

What is the pig's favorite motorcycle?

A Hogly Davidson

What is the pig's favorite auto race?

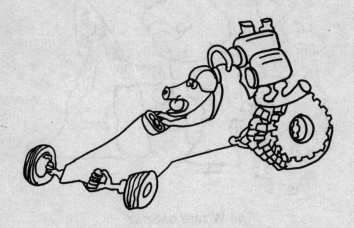

The In-de-ham-apple-is 500

What is the little pig's favorite cookie?

A Pig Newton

What is the little pig's favorite fairy tale?

The Wizard of Snoz

What is the little pig's favorite game?

Pig-up sticks

What are the little pig's two favorite movies?

Sty Wars and *The Hampire Strikes Back*

DINING OUT

A sit-down dinner for four

A buffet

FAVORITE PIG TALES

Rapigzel

Swinederella

Hams Brinker

AND OF COURSE
THE THREE LITTLE PIGS

Once upon a time,
three little pigs
had trouble building
their houses.

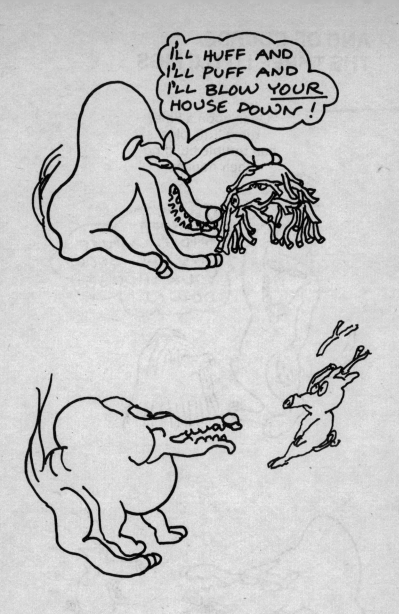

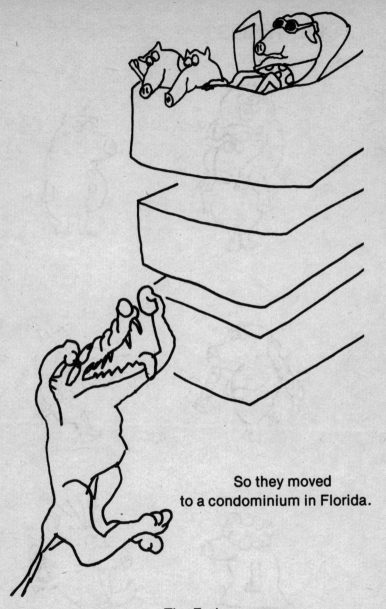

So they moved
to a condominium in Florida.

The End

PIG TERMS

1.

2.

3.

4.

5.

6.

Hamswers

1. Piggyback

2. A road hog

3. Pigtails

4. A pig in a poke

5. Pig curls

6. Hog wild

Squeals of Delight

What kinds of pigs are these?

1.

2.

3.

4.

5.

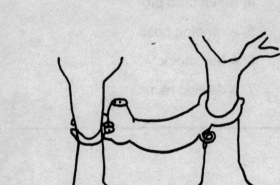

6.

7.

Hamswers

1) A pig in love

2) A coin operated pig

3) A pig with a stopped-up nose

4) An electric pig

5) A running boar

6) A hammock

7) A deviled ham

A pig curling its tail

BILLY FATSON'S
BIG MISTAKE

THE GREAT PORKOLA

APPLAUSE

MORE GREAT AND FAMOUS PIGS

What famous President pig crossed the Smellaware?

George Washingham

What famous conqueror pig crossed the Alps?

Hammibal

What President pig was a famous nothern general?

Ulysses S. Grunt

What famous pig defeated Napoleham Bone-a-pork?

The Duke of Wellingham

What pig was a famous ruler of Germany?

Kaiser Wilham II

What two pigs were famous rulers of England?

Pigtoria and Alboar

What famous pig monster is six feet tall and sewn together?

Frankenswine

What famous pig's nose got longer when he told a lie?

Pignocchio

What pig is a famous superhero?

Superham—the Man of Squeal

What pig was a famous strongman in the Bible?

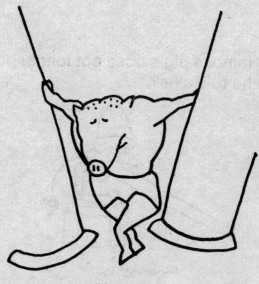

Hamson

What pig was a famous rohamtic poet?

Omar Khayham

What is the pig's favorite TV game show?

Squeal of Fortune

About the Author

MIKE THALER is known as America's Riddle King. He is the creator of Letterman, the popular "Electric Company" character, and has earned a fine reputation as author and illustrator of over eighty children's books, ranging from original riddle and joke books to fables, picture books, and *I Can Reads*. In addition, Mike has designed games for Playspaces, software for Mindscape, made recordings for Scholastic and Caedmon Records and appeared in TV videos. The *Saturday Review* has called him "one of the most creative people in children's books today."

In addition to his work with children's books, Mike spends much of his time sculpting, drawing, and song-writing. He is a sought-after speaker and has given many programs and workshops for children and adults across the country.

Above all, he believes in creativity—in himself and in others. "That is," says Mike, "my life and my work."